The Ragdoll

Annual
2000

What's Inside?

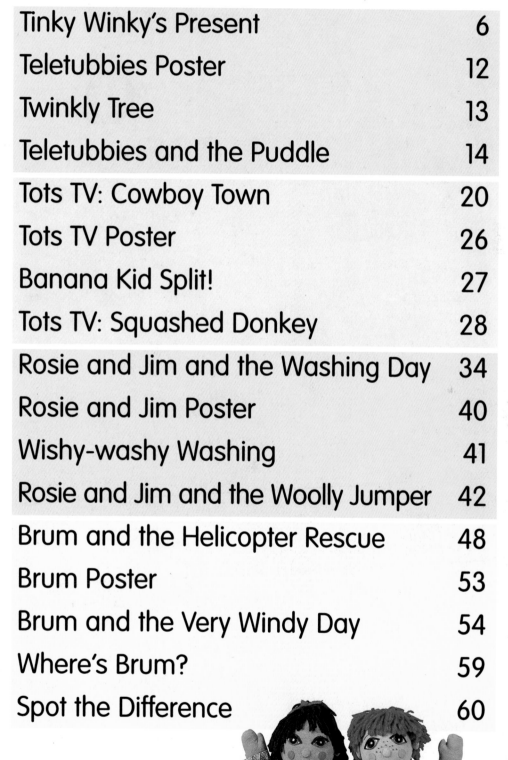

Tinky Winky's Present

One day in Teletubbyland, Tinky Winky had a present.

Tinky Winky present!

Look! Present!

tinkle twinkle

Tinky Winky ran all the way home with the present.

tinkle tinkle

Run home with present!

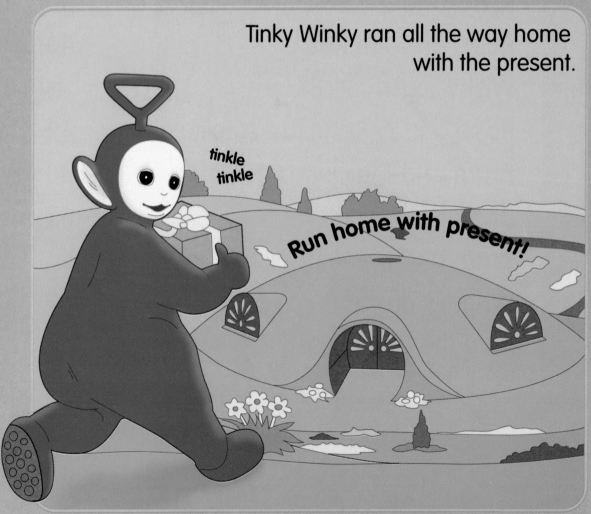

Tinky Winky opened
his present.

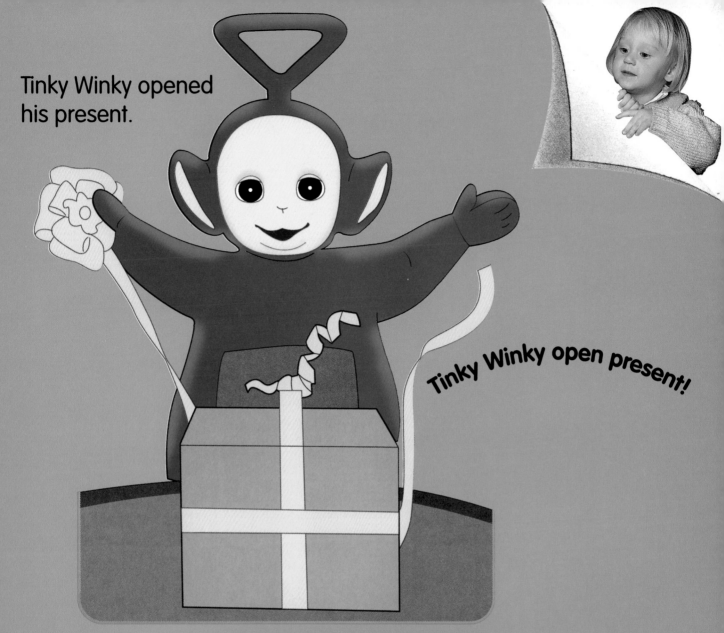

Tinky Winky open present!

Ooooooh! What's that?

tinkle
twinkle

7

It was a star.

Star! Ooooh!

But then the star floated away. Tinky Winky wondered where the star was going.

Tinky Winky followed the star.

Where star going?

Tinky Winky follow star!

8

The star floated over Po.

Then the star
floated over Dipsy
and Laa-Laa.

The star floated away.

9

Tinky Winky, Dipsy, Laa-Laa and Po followed the star...

...all the way...

...to the Christmas tree.

Happy Christmas, Teletubbies!

tinkle
twinkle

Happy Christmas!

Twinkly Tree

Twinkle, Twinkle
Little Star
How I wonder
what you are?

★ The children are decorating their Christmas tree. You can help by colouring the tree and putting a star on top of it!
★ Draw on lots more decorations or make some really sparkly ones out of silver foil, milk bottle tops or tinsel!
★ What would you like to find under the tree?

13

The Puddle

One day in Teletubbyland,

a cloud appeared.

It began to rain.

The rain made a puddle.

Along came Laa-Laa.

Laa-laa-li-laa

Laa-Laa stepped in the puddle.

Ooooh!

Eeeeyyyyrrr!

Laa-Laa step in puddle!

Along came Dipsy.

Bup-a-tum, bup-a-tum, bup-a-tum!

15

Dipsy stepped around the puddle.

Oooh! Dipsy step around puddle!

Along came Tinky Winky.

Pinkle Winkle Tinky Winky!

Tinky Winky stepped over the puddle.

Ooooh!

Tinky Winky step over puddle!

Along came Po.

Fi-dit fi-dit fi-dit!

Po rode her scooter through the puddle.

Uh oh!

18

Eeeeyyyrrr! Po through puddle. Eeeerrryyyrrr! Po through puddle!

The Teletubbies love Po.

Big Hug!

The Teletubbies love each other very much.

Cowboy Town

One day, Cowboy Tom rode into Cowboy Town.

"I'm Tom the big bad baddy," he sang. "I've come riding into town to see what's to be had. Tom the big bad baddy! Yiii-har!"

"Look. That's a picture of me, that is," said Big Bad Tom. "Oh - someone's coming. I'd better hide!"

I'm Tiny the banana kid. Bananas is my game.
I deliver the bananas: that's how I got my name.
I deliver the bananas, because that's what I do best.
I'm Tiny the banana kid, the fastest banana in the West!"

"Bananas!" said Big
Bad Tom. "I'm going to steal me some of them."

"Bonjour! Je suis Tilly, le shérif, et ceci est mon cheval," said Tilly.

"Oh, no! It's Sheriff Tilly and her horse!"

"It's Sheriff Tilly!" cried Tiny. "She catches all the baddies! Hello, Sheriff Tilly. Hello, horse!"
"Attention! Big Bad Tom est en ville!" said Tilly.
"Big Bad Tom's in town?" said Tiny.

"Attention, Tiny!" said Sheriff Tilly. "Au revoir!"
"Yes, Tilly, I'll watch out!" Tiny promised.
"Bye! Cor - I'd better watch my bananas."

"Too late! Hand over your bananas!" cried Big Bad Tom. "Hand over my bananas? Why?" asked Tiny. "I'm Tom the big bad baddy, I am," said Tom.

"Oh, all right then. If you're the big bad baddy, then here are my bananas. You're such a big bad baddy, Tom."

"I know. Ha, ha!" laughed Big Bad Tom.

"Oh, no. Big Bad Tom has taken all my bananas.
What am I going to do now?
Oh, look! There's Sheriff Tilly and her horse."

"Oooh, Sheriff Tilly! Guess what!" cried Tiny.
"Tom the big, bad baddy has taken all my bananas!"
"Oh, là là!" said Tilly. "Allez! Il faut que nous le poursuivions!"
"Yes, we must chase after him!" said Tiny.
"Oh, quick, Tilly!"

"Oh, no, you've caught me!" said Big Bad Tom.

"Yep, we've caught you!" said Tiny. "Hand over those bananas!"

"Hey, Tots, I'm not the big bad baddy any more, am I?" said Tom. "No, Tom. It was a good game, though, wasn't it?"

Banana Kid Split!

Before you begin, you will need:
A banana • A plate • A spoon • A grown-up!

★ Cut the banana in half and place on
a plate.

★ Add 2–3 large scoops of ice-cream.

★ Stick 2 flakes into the ice cream.

★ Pour raspberry sauce or hundreds and
thousands all over and squirt with cream.
Now take your spoon and eat!!!!

Tots tv
Squashed Donkey

One day, Tilly was busy making a model of Donkey out of dough.

Tiny was doing some housework. "Polishing, cleaning, polishing, cleaning," sang Tiny. "Oh Tom," said Tiny, "I'm polishing the stairs. Would you like to join in?"

"Oh, all right then," said Tom. "You do the straight bits and I'll do the roundy bits, all right?"

"Tom, Tiny!" called Tilly. "Regardez le modèle que j'ai fait!" "Oh, hello, Tilly," said Tiny. "What's that you've made?" "What is it, Tilly?" asked Tom.

"C'est Donkey!" said Tilly.
"Erm...it's lovely, Tilly," said Tom.
"Tilly, that's brilliant," said Tiny.

"Deux oreilles vertes," said Tilly.
"Two green ears," said Tiny.

"Le corps jaune," said Tilly.
"A yellow body," said Tom,
trying not to giggle.

"Quatres petites jambes rouges," said Tilly.
"Four little red legs," said Tom.

"Et une petite queue verte," said Tilly.
"And a little green tail!" giggled Tiny.

"It's just like Donkey, Tilly," said Tom.
"Oh yes, it looks just like Donkey,"
said Tiny, and he gave
the little dough model
a kiss.

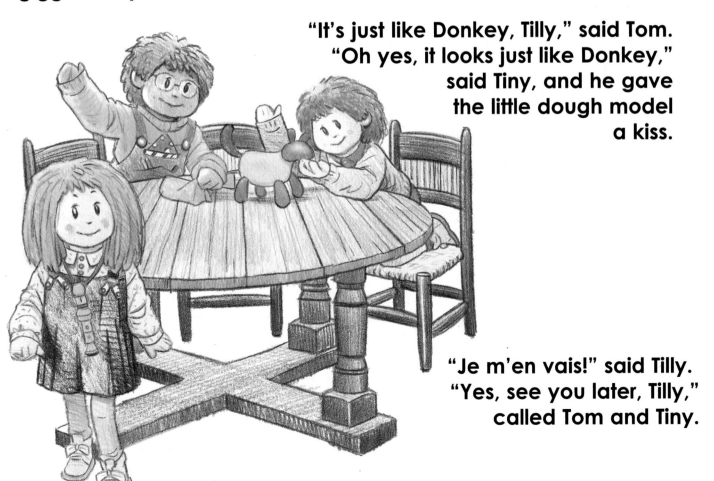

"Je m'en vais!" said Tilly.
"Yes, see you later, Tilly,"
called Tom and Tiny.

29

"Tom, do you want to do some more polishing?" asked Tiny. "No, Tiny," said Tom. "I'm going to read a book, I am."
"Oh," said Tiny. "Actually, I'd like to read a book, but I'm just going to polish the table first. Um, Tom, could you get me a book with a story while you're there?"
"Oh, all right then," said Tom.

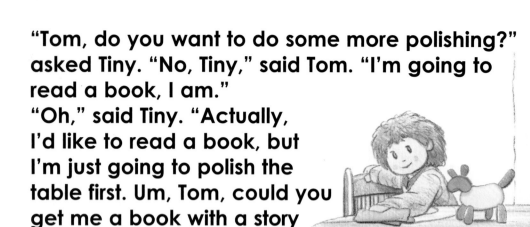

"Ooh, I'd better move this," said Tiny. "We don't want any accidents. I'll put it on the chair while I polish."

"Here you are, Tiny," said Tom. "I've got a book for you and one for me."

"Thanks, Tom," said Tiny. "That looks nice."

"Shall I sit down here? Then we can read our books together," said Tom.
"Yes, let's read our books together," said Tiny.

30

"Oooh!" said Tom.
"What was that?"

"Oh, Tom!" said Tiny.
"You've sat on Tilly's
donkey!"
"Oh, no! What was
that doing on my
chair?" said Tom.

"Tom, look it's all squashed!"

"Oh, no! Well, that was a silly place to
put it, Tiny, you big banana!" said Tom.

"But I didn't know you were going to sit
on it, Tom, you big tomato!" said Tiny.

"Banana!"
"Tomato!"

"Oh, Tilly's
coming!" said Tom.
"She's going to
see her donkey's
all squashed
now," said Tiny.
"She's going to
be really upset."

"Don't tell her I did it," said Tom.
"No, don't tell her I did it," said Tiny.

                    "Bonjour, Tiny! Bonjour, Tom!" said Tilly.

"Oh, hello Tilly," said Tom and Tiny.
"Regardez!" said Tilly.
"Oh, Tilly, what a lovely flower!" said Tom.

"Tiny, Tom, où est mon âne?" asked Tilly.
"Oh, your Donkey," said Tom. "Well...erm..."
"Well, Tom sat on it and squashed it!"
said Tiny.
"Tiny, I didn't!"
"Yes you did, Tom. You sat on it!" said
Tiny.
"Yeah, but you put it on my chair!" said
Tom.

"You great tomato!"
"Banana!"

32

"Regardez! L'âne ressemble à ma fleur!" said Tilly.
"It does look just like a flower," said Tom.
"Yeah, it's a donkey flower!" said Tiny.

The Tots took the flower to show their friend, Donkey.

"Regarde, Donkey!" said Tilly.
"Yeah, look, Donkey!" said Tiny. "It's a lovely donkey flower."

Rosie and Jim™
Washing Day

1. "Oh dear, it's washing day again," said Tootle. "Let's see...whites over there...blue over here..."

2. "It's washing day again, Jim," whispered Rosie. "Smelly socks day again...Pooooooh!" said Jim.

3. "In with the soap," said Neil. "Oops, a bit too much!"

4. "Rub a dub dub, give it a scrub, make it nice and clean!" sang Rosie and Jim.

5. "Now I need to rinse everything," said Neil.

6. "Rinse, rinse, give it a rinse, wash those bubbles out!" sang Rosie and Jim.

7. "Good," said Neil. "Now all I have to do is peg everything up to dry!"

8. "We'll help Tootle, Jim," said Rosie. "Yes, with the washing line," said Jim.

9. "That looks fine to me," said Neil, testing the washing line. "Woooooaaaaah, Rosie. Hold on tight!" said Jim. "I am holding tight, Jim," said Rosie.

10. "Pull, Jim!" said Rosie. "Pull!"
"I am pulling, Rosie!" said Jim. "Oooops!"

11. "Look at Tootle's nice dirty laundry, Jim!" said Rosie. "Yes, lovely and dirty, Rosie!" "Quack!" said Duck. "Duck thinks we should wash it again for Tootle," said Rosie.

12. "Rub a dub dub, give it a scrub. Wash it nice and clean!" sang Rosie and Jim.

13. "Rinse, rinse, give it a rinse. Wash those bubbles out!" they sang.

14. Rosie gave the end of the washing line to Duck. "Hold this a minute, Duck," she said.

15. "Peg, peg, peg it all out," sang Rosie and Jim. "Peg it all out to dry!"

16. "There. All pegged out to dry!" said Rosie. "Yes, all nice and clean," said Jim, stepping back. "Wooooooaaaaa..."

17. "There. I'm a nice and dirty Jim," said Jim. "Yes," giggled Rosie. "A lovely and dirty Jim!"

18. "Rub a dub dub, give Jim a scrub, make him nice and clean!" sang Rosie.

19. "Peg, peg, peg Jim out, peg Jim out to dry," sang Rosie. "Thank you, Rosie," said Jim. "Weeeee!"

20. Suddenly, Duck saw Neil coming back. "Quack!" he went - and lost the end of the washing line!

21. "Come on, Jim, Tootle's coming!"
"Oh, no! I don't believe it!" said Neil. "I'm going to have to start all over again!"

22. "Oh, Rosie!" said Jim. "Jim!" giggled Rosie.

Wishy-washy Washing

★ Help hang the washing on the line. Draw round the dotted lines, then finish colouring the pictures.

41

The Woolly Jumper

One day, the Ragdoll was quietly travelling down the canal. A family with two young children was walking along the towpath. They were all wearing matching jumpers.

Rosie and Jim were secretly looking out of the hatch.

"Look, Rosie!" said Jim, pointing to the family. "Woolly jumpers!"

"Just like Tootle's!" giggled Rosie.

42

Just then Neil looked and saw the family, too.

"Those people are all wearing jumpers just like mine!" said Neil to himself. Then he called across. "Hello! Excuse me, but could you tell me where you got your woolly jumpers?"

"Over there - at the knitting factory," they told Neil. He thanked them and turned the Ragdoll towards the bank. "I think I'll go and take a look."

Neil tied up the Ragdoll and then went off to visit the knitting factory.

"Look, Jim," said Rosie. "Tootle's caught his jumper on the door catch."

"Let's follow the long, long wool, Rosie," laughed Jim.

"Follow the long, long wool!"
"Wool wool, follow the wool!"

Neil was so interested in the factory building that he didn't look where he was going - and he bumped straight into a man carrying a pile of jumpers. Jumpers fell everywhere.

"Oh, I'm sorry," said Neil, and bent to help the man pick up the jumpers. "Is this where the jumpers are made?"

"Yes, this is a knitting factory. I'm Stephen, the manager. Would you like to come in and look round?" said the man.

"I'd love to," said Neil.

Rosie and Jim secretly followed them into the factory, winding up the long, long trail of wool from Neil's jumper as they went.

Stephen showed Neil where the jumpers were made.

"This is the big machine which knits the jumpers," he said.

"Very clever," said Neil.

Rosie and Jim peeked at the knitting machine, too.

"Knitting machine, Rosie," whispered Jim. "It's knitting a jumper."

"Isn't it clever, Jim?" said Rosie.

Then Stephen took Neil to where the machinists were working.

"This is where the seams are sewn together," said Stephen.

"Sewing the woolly jumper, Jim," whispered Rosie.

"Sewing it all together!" said Jim.

Stephen held up a newly finished jumper. "So, this is the finished jumper, Neil," said Stephen.

"Thank you very much, Stephen, I've really enjoyed my visit."

Just then, Stephen noticed something strange about Neil's jumper. It was very short! "Um, Neil, look at your jumper," he said.

"Oh, no!" cried Neil. "How did that happen?

"Oh, no, Jim," said Rosie. "Look at Tootle's jumper!"

"How did that happen?" said Jim.

45

"Here, you can have this one if you like," said Stephen, holding out the finished jumper.

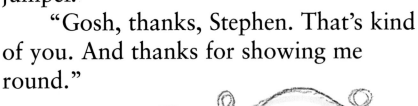

"Gosh, thanks, Stephen. That's kind of you. And thanks for showing me round."

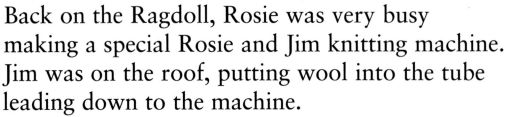

Back on the Ragdoll, Rosie was very busy making a special Rosie and Jim knitting machine. Jim was on the roof, putting wool into the tube leading down to the machine.

"Duck wants to know if his new jumper is ready yet, Rosie," said Jim.

"Nearly, Jim," said Rosie. "I just need to adjust my controls..."

"Here comes your new jumper, Duck. Here it comes..."

"Here it comes, Duck," said Rosie. "A nice new woolly..."

"Quack," said Duck.

"...BANANA! Oh dear, Duck. I just need to tweak the controls a bit."

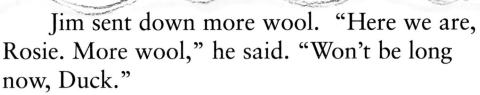

Jim sent down more wool. "Here we are, Rosie. More wool," he said. "Won't be long now, Duck."

"Here it comes, Duck," called Rosie. Your nice new woolly...

... SAUSAGES! Oh, no."

"QUACK!" said Duck. "Quack, quack!"

"Quick, Rosie, Tootle's coming back!" said Jim, tossing the rest of the wool over Duck. They quickly scrambled back to their places inside the boat.

"Hello there, Duck," said Tootle. "How do you like my nice new jumper? Hey, Duck, you've got a jumper, too!"

Neil looked a bit closer. "Mmmm. It looks like wool from my old jumper. Strange."

I've no one to be my sweetheart, Brum.

I'll give my chocolates to Micky. **Wait!**

Oh, no. He's gone!

Don't worry - I'll go and find him.

Brum soon caught up with Micky.

Hey, Brum! Have you seen the Lollipop Lady? I want her to be my sweetheart.

She's looking for you, Micky. Come on, let's go and find her.

Look! There she is!

49

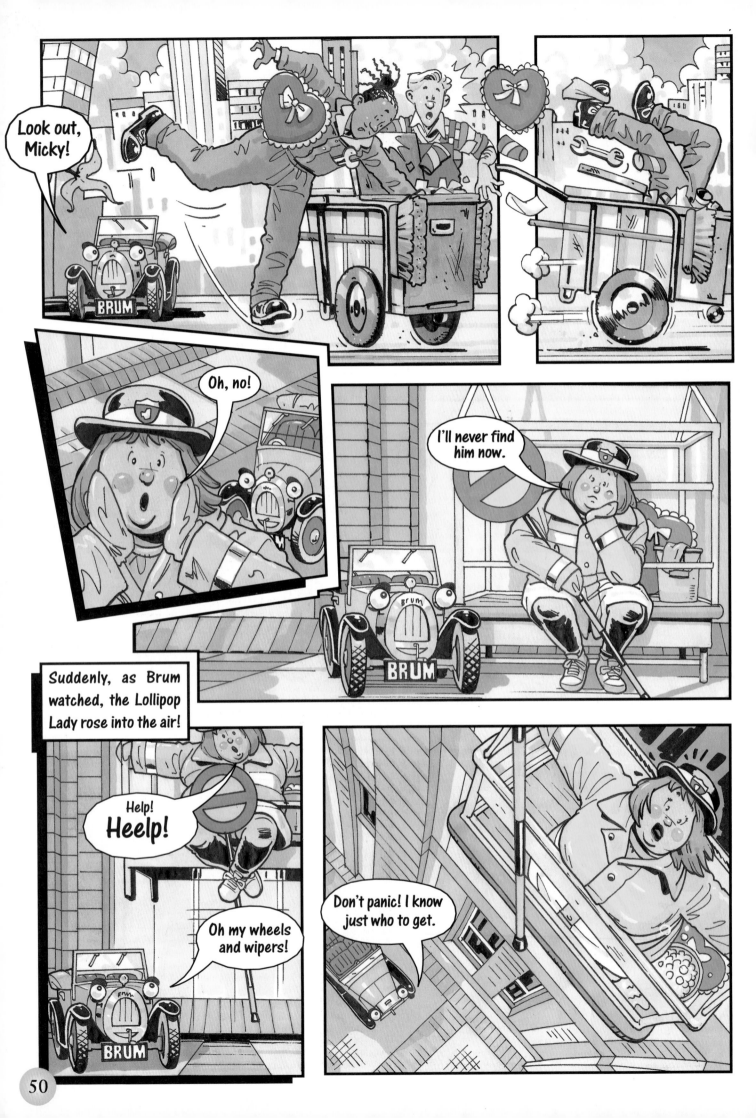

Brum brummed away as fast as he could to the airport.

Of course I'll help, Brum.

Hooray! I'm flying! Brum to the rescue.

Brum flew over the Lollipop Lady.

Hang on tight to my bumper!

Safely on the ground again.

Hooray for Brum!

Brum™

The Very Windy Day

One day Brum was brum, brum, brumming along the pavement in the Big Town, when suddenly...

WHOOOSH!

...a big gust of wind swept down the road and blew him right up to the Lollipop Lady.

Ooh! Sorry, Lollipop Lady!

Watch out, Brum. The wind is playing tricks today.

Along the road Brum met the paperboy.

Watch out! The wind's playing tricks today.

Thanks, Brum, I will.

At Mrs Doolally's house.

Watch out! The wind's playing tricks today.

Thanks, Brum, I will. But it's good for the washing.

Waaaaaaah!

At the Ladidah's house.

Hello, Mr and Mrs Lahdidah. Watch out for the wind!

Over in the park Brum's friend Vicky Spoon came by.

Come and play frisbee, Brum.

Cor! That looks really clever.

Suddenly...

55

Where's Brum?

Spot the Difference

Can you spot five differences between these two Brum pictures?
The answers are at the bottom of this page.

More

Favourites

Look out for these top-selling titles in all good bookshops.
Super Rhyming Reader/Sticker Poster Books.
The rhymes are left for you to complete with lots of silly or sensible stickers.
Only £2.50 each.

Silly Sausage
Sticker Poster Book
ISBN 07498 37306

Noodle Noggin
Sticker Poster Book
ISBN 07498 37314

Plus hours of fun drawing Rosie & Jim and Tots characters in colourful scenes,
with the help of these super Stencil Books. Only £3.99 each.

Rosie & Jim
Stencil Book
ISBN 07498 36857

Tots TV
Story Stencils
ISBN 07498 36873

Plus

**Tilly, Tom and Tiny's
BIG TREASURE ADVENTURE**
The Tots take over the legendary
ship, the *Bounty* and, while sailing,
find a treasure map in a bottle.
64 pages of adventure as the Tots
find their 'Treasure Island'.

ISBN 07498 38981 Only £4.99

If you have any difficulty finding these titles please contact Egmont World Limited, Deanway Technology Centre, Wilmslow Road, Handforth, Cheshire, SK9 3FB. Telephone 01625 650011.